S.O.S.
SOCIETY OF SUBSTITUTES
The Great Escape

Enjoy More Great S.O.S. Adventures!

HARPER **Chapters**

By Alan Katz

Illustrated by Alex Lopez

HARPER

An Imprint of HarperCollins*Publishers*

To all teachers—you are true superheroes

—Alan Katz

Library of Congress Control Number: 2020934478
ISBN 978-0-06-290928-2 — ISBN 978-0-06-290929-9 (paperback)

Typography by Corina Lupp
21 22 23 24   PC/LSCC   10 9 8 7 6 5 4 3 2

First Edition

TABLE OF CONTENTS

CHAPTER 1

It Begins

IN 311B, WE STUDY
MATH, SCIENCE, AND HISTORY.
THOUGH WHY THERE'S
NO 311A IS A STRANGE AND
CURIOUS MYSTERY.

Mrs. Baltman always started the week with a funny message. The second graders in Room 311B looked forward to her Monday signs. Some even wished she would greet them with a new one every day.

And this message was both funny and mysterious. No one had any idea why there wasn't a Room 311A.

Not even Milton Worthy—and he usually had a smart answer for everything. No, today Milton walked into the classroom and didn't even look at the funny message. Because today, Milton knew he had a job to do.

It's Monday, and on Mondays I have a very special, important job, he thought to himself. *I just wish I could remember what that job is.*

Milton looked around the room for a clue. The maps were neatly folded. The paper towel holder was filled. And then, Milton's eyes landed on Noah, the class ferret, in his super escape-proof cage.

NOAH

"Hey, ferret-face!" Milton called out. Noah, who had been doing whatever it is tired, bored, hungry ferrets do, perked right up.

Oh yeah, Monday is the day I refill Noah's num-nums! Milton told himself.

"I'll be right there, pal," he said to the ferret. "But first, I gotta hang up my coat and unpack my backpack. Then I gotta three-hole-punch my homework and jump shot my lunch box into the cooler."

Milton missed his shot.

He missed again.

And again.

After six tries, Milton's lunch box still wasn't in the classroom cooler.

He moved closer. And closer. And closer, until . . .

"Slam dunk by Milton Worthy! The crowd goes wild!" he yelled as he stuffed the lunch box into the cooler.

Noah made a noise that sounded like, "Ahem . . ."

Milton ran to Noah's cage and opened the door, which wasn't easy. Milton had to slide the slide, unlatch the latch, lift the lever, and press-turn the knob just to open the slot to feed him. (Because Noah had escaped several times before, the class had built a new, multilock cage to keep Noah safe.)

"Here you go! Tasty num-nums for Noah! Delicious fresh water too! Enjoy your meal!"

Milton was having so much fun that he didn't realize that other kids had entered the classroom.

"Hey, Milton," Sarah Rosario laughed. "Have any num-nums for *me*?"

"I was just making sure Noah is well fed," he said as he put the ferret food away.

The kids were still laughing as they sat down to wait for Mrs. Baltman.

"Good morning, one and all," the teacher boomed as she entered. "I'm looking forward to a wonderful week! How about all of you?"

"Let's start the day with some silent reading," the teacher said.

Everyone took out a book as Mrs. Baltman started grading math test papers.

Milton, however, couldn't concentrate on reading. He had a nagging feeling in the back of his mind that he'd forgotten something. But what?

A few moments later, Sarah whispered to Milton from the desk next to his.

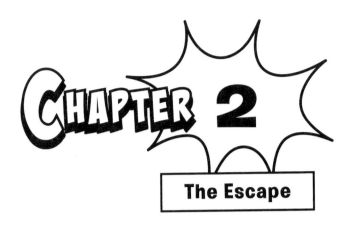

The Escape

Indeed, Noah's cage slot was open. The ferret was gone!

Milton knew that Noah had *escaped* because Milton had forgotten to close the door. He had not press-turned the knob, lowered the lever, latched the latch, and slid the slide to lock him in.

"Oh my, oh my," Mrs. Baltman gasped. "The ferret is loose again?"

"Don't worry, Mrs. Baltman," Milton told her.

"Noah always comes back. Remember last time? Noah may have taken some salami from David Tessler's backpack, but he didn't get out of the classroom. We got him back in his cage eventually."

"But the new cage was supposed to . . . Last time was so . . . We must stop the ferret from . . . I mean, oh my goodness!"

Mrs. Baltman wasn't making much sense. She sputtered out a few more words, then started coughing.

And coughing. And coughing. And coughing.

It was the worst fake cough Milton had ever heard—and Milton knew a lot about faking a cough. He himself had done it once . . . or twice . . . or perhaps thirty-seven times . . . *But why would Mrs. Baltman fake a cough?*

Finally, Mrs. Baltman took a sip of water and tried to "cough out" instructions.

"Re . . . *cough* . . . re . . . *cough* . . . re . . . *cough* . . ."

"*Respect your classmates?*" said Sarah, trying to help by finishing Mrs. Baltman's thought.

Mrs. Baltman shook her head *no*.

"Re . . . *cough* . . . re . . . *cough* . . ."

"*Recycle* cans and bottles?" said Max Goen, also trying to help.

Mrs. Baltman shook her head again.

"Re . . . *cough* . . . re . . . *cough* . . ."

"*Remarkable* job on your math test, Morgan?" Milton's closest friend, Morgan Zhou, guessed.

The teacher took another sip of water and managed to utter . . .

Mrs. Baltman continued coughing as she waved everyone to the back door so they could file out for early recess. Recess was usually the best part of the day, but no one felt like taking a break since school hadn't even really started yet.

"This is so weird," Max said. "We *just* took our seats."

Sarah agreed. "Recess is supposed to be a break, but we haven't *done* any work yet. How

are we supposed to enjoy taking a break from doing *nothing*?"

But Milton was less concerned about the sudden recess, and more confused about why Mrs. Baltman had started fake-coughing when she learned the ferret was gone. After all, fake coughing coming from a *teacher* is just . . . weird.

"We need to go back inside!" Milton exclaimed.

"Yeah," David Tessler added. "I don't feel like playing anyway." David then checked his own forehead to see if he had a high fever—it wasn't like him to say something like that.

"We need to help Mrs. Baltman find Noah," Milton said.

So everyone ended their much-too-early recess. But when they walked back inside, they discovered . . .

. . . Mrs. Baltman was gone! And in her place was . . .

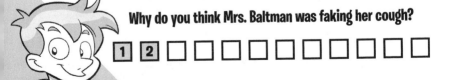

Why do you think Mrs. Baltman was faking her cough?

1 2 ☐ ☐ ☐ ☐ ☐ ☐ ☐ ☐ ☐ ☐

The Surprise Sub!

Milton's mother, Mrs. Rose Worthy!

"Whaaat? What is she doing here?" Milton asked.

"Mrs. Baltman couldn't stop coughing, so I'll be your substitute teacher today."

Everyone in the class said, "Good morning, Mrs. Worthy." Except, that is, for Milton. He said, "But . . . but . . . but . . ."

"But nothing," Mrs. Worthy said. "Everyone, please take your seats."

Mrs. Worthy started talking to the class. But Milton didn't hear anything she was saying. He was too busy trying to figure out what was going on . . . and ignoring his friends' comments.

Milton's mom got right down to business, giving out a series of very odd assignments.

"Blueprints! I need the school's blueprints! Immediately. Row three, line up and hurry to the main office," Mrs. Worthy said.

Milton thought that was strange. *Why on earth would she need to know the layout of the whole school?*

"Row two, please search the room for Noah,"

Mrs. Worthy said. "He can't have gotten far."

Milton thought that was strange as well. *Why would his mother be so anxious to find Noah?*

"And make sure to alert the rest of the school!"

Everyone got right to work, except for Milton's row. Mrs. Worthy had not given them an assignment. So they sat and watched the rest of the class work.

Milton's mom took a little green notebook out of her purse and started firing off questions.

"Morgan, has Noah been sleeping extra-long hours?"

"Mrs. Worthy," Morgan Zhou said. "*All* hours have sixty minutes in them. How could he possibly sleep extra-long ones?"

"What I meant was: Has Noah been sleeping *a lot*?" Mrs. Worthy asked.

"A lot for people? Or a lot for ferrets?" Morgan wanted to know.

Max jumped in.

"I read that ferrets sleep up to eighteen hours a day, Mrs. Worthy," he said. "That's six thousand five hundred seventy hours a year!"

"Good math, young man," Mrs. Worthy told him. "But I'd really like to know about any odd behavior."

"My brother ate an ice cream cone topped with roast beef," David said. "That was pretty odd—even for him."

"I mean *Noah's* odd behavior. Anyone?"

No one could think of a single thing. Noah had seemed like a pretty normal, boring ferret.

Morgan tapped Milton on the shoulder.

"Hey, Milton, why is your mom so interested in Noah?" Morgan wanted to know.

"I . . . um . . . well . . . er . . . you see . . . ," Milton responded. He really had no idea, so he shrugged a shrug so big that his shoulders almost covered his ears.

"*Anything? Anything at all unusual?*" Mrs. Worthy repeated. "Come on, people!"

The truth was, Milton could think of only one thing that was unusual in the classroom. It was . . .

. . . how interested his mom was in the missing ferret.

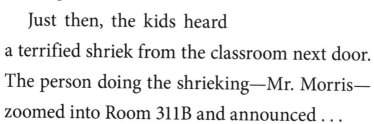

Just then, the kids heard a terrified shriek from the classroom next door. The person doing the shrieking—Mr. Morris— zoomed into Room 311B and announced . . .

CHAPTER 4

Recess, Again?

Mrs. Worthy kept asking about Noah until the kids from row three returned with the blueprints. Mrs. Worthy grabbed the poster-sized sheets and then told the class, "I need to carefully review these blueprints. So everybody go outside for recess—"

The whole class started to object.

Max spoke up. "It's only nine twenty-seven, and we've already had one recess today.

Plus, we usually don't go to recess until one. That's three hours, thirty-three minutes from now."

"Good math again, young man," Mrs. Worthy told him. "But I said *recess now.* N-O-W. GO!"

"Mrs. Worthy, remember what they say," Max said. "All play and no work makes Jack a dull boy."

But Mrs. Worthy wasn't changing her mind. So, once again, everyone in the second-grade

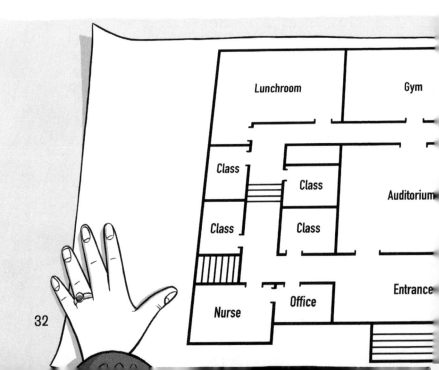

class shuffled outside.

Everyone *except* Milton, that is.

Instead, Milton hid inside the coat closet in the back of the room. The other kids were so busy complaining about playing outside that they didn't notice he wasn't there. And his mother was so busy reviewing the blueprints that she didn't even look up to notice that Milton hadn't gone with his friends.

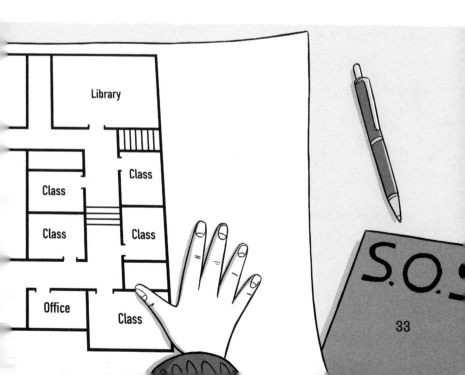

Peeking through a crack in the coat closet door, Milton watched his mom scribble notes in her little green notebook.

Milton told himself that this day was setting the all-time record for weirdness: Two recesses before ten, two classroom pets missing, one teacher gone home with a "cough," and his mother was the substitute teacher. And weirdest of all . . .

. . . Milton Worthy had skipped out on playing kickball to spy on his mother from inside a coat closet that smelled like David Tessler's lunch. From his hiding spot, he saw his mother check to make sure the coast was clear before taking out a giant helmet and putting it on her head.

CHAPTER 5

Calling Headquarters

Milton could see that his mother was wearing a football-style helmet with a wireless microphone, a speaker, and a giant antenna that extended from the top. The letters S.O.S. were painted on the side of it.

S.O.S.? What in the world does S.O.S. stand for? Milton wondered.

He didn't have to wait long to find out. His mother pressed a button on the side of the helmet and said, "This is Agent W, super-sub, calling Society of Substitutes headquarters . . ."

. . . REQUESTING TO SPEAK TO CHIEFMAN.

Milton heard a voice respond. "Yes, R.W. Chief Chiefman here."

Milton almost toppled out of the closet as he listened to Chief Chiefman tell his mom what was going on. As it turned out:

Upon learning that Noah had escaped, Mrs. Baltman faked a cough so that she could go home sick. (Aha! Milton *had guessed* that it was fake!) That activated the Society of Substitutes's warning systems, which called Milton's mom. Her job now was to do whatever it took to . . .

. . . stop an evil genius who was planning to take over the school, the town, *and* the world . . .

. . . and that evil genius was . . .

. . . none other than . . .

Congratulations. You've read 2,249 words. Way to go!

1 2 3 4 5 ☐ ☐ ☐ ☐ ☐ ☐ ☐

CHAPTER 6

Evil Pet Island

. . . Noah the ferret!

Upon learning that Noah the class ferret was an evil genius bent on taking over the world, Milton nearly yelped out loud. He had to put both hands over his mouth to keep from giving away his hiding spot.

Milton couldn't believe what he was seeing: his mother was a superhero. He rubbed his eyes.

He couldn't believe what he was hearing: she

was the only thing standing between freedom and ferret world domination. He rubbed his ears.

And Milton couldn't believe how incredibly hungry seeing and hearing all this made him. He rubbed his tummy.

Seeing no other option, Milton plucked a pack of juicy chicken wings out of David Tessler's backpack. He shoved the bag of wings into his sweatshirt pocket—to eat later, when he didn't have to be so quiet.

"Okay, Agent W, here's the complete capture-the-evil-ferret plan," the voice coming from the helmet said.

"Ready, Chief," Mrs. Worthy said.

"Each time Noah escaped, he always got back into his cage before we could figure out what he

was up to," the Chief said.

"But you have a theory now, Chief?" Mrs. Worthy said.

"We think Noah wants to teleport the school to the E.P.I.," the Chief said.

"The E.P.I., sir?" Mrs. Worthy asked.

"Evil Pet Island," the Chief told her. "Noah wants to teleport the school, the town, and the world . . . there. He and his evil pet pals are seeking complete control!"

"My goodness!" Mrs. Worthy exclaimed.

Milton had seen people and objects teleported on science-fiction shows. If there was a silver lining in Noah's evil plan, it was that teleporting doesn't *harm* anything. Things just disappear from one location and appear in another.

The Chief continued, "We need to capture that ferret."

"Yes, Chief—and then what?"

"Get him back in his cage, and make sure the kids don't forget to lock it after feeding him," the Chief said.

"The school, the town, the world, and my aunt Pauline are counting on you."

"Your aunt Pauline, sir?" Mrs. Worthy asked.

"Yes. Her favorite show, *Wow! That's Talent*, is on every Monday night. And if Noah takes over, she'll miss the final episode and never find out who wins the one-hundred-million-dollar grand prize."

Milton took a deep breath. Over the last few minutes, he'd learned that his mother was a secret superhero, that his classroom pet was an evil genius, and that Aunt Pauline really enjoyed *Wow! That's Talent*.

Now I've seen and heard it all . . . , Milton told himself.

But he hadn't.

Not by a long shot.

CHAPTER 7

The S.O.E.P.?

After signing off with the Chief, Milton's mother took off her S.O.S. helmet and placed it in the Helmet Recharge-o-Matic.

Milton hoped his mother would take a bath-room break. Or go for coffee. Or do *something* that would cause her to leave the room so he could sneak out of the back closet.

But she wasn't going anywhere, because . . .

. . . Noah, the evil genius ferret, zoomed into the room! He was wearing a helmet like the one Mom had been wearing. Except that instead of S.O.S., the letters *S.O.E.P.* were painted on it.

Remarkably, Milton instantly knew it stood for Society of Evil Pets.

Noah looks so cute in his itty-bitty helmet, Milton thought. Then he remembered that there was nothing cute about a creature that wanted to teleport the whole world to an evil island.

Noah whooshed around the room and leapt up onto the teacher's desk. He knocked Milton's mom's helmet off its charging stand and onto the floor.

Milton's mom grabbed her helmet and what Milton recognized as the desktop pencil sharpener and blasted a blinding light ray at Noah.

No wonder that thing always gets my pencil tips so sharp, Milton thought.

But Noah was fast. He ducked every blast Mom fired.

Next, Mrs. Worthy tossed an eraser grenade

at Noah. It hit the floor and exploded, missing Noah but wiping the chalkboard as clean as it'd ever been.

Noah stood up on his hind legs and spun around like he was ready to fight.

Then he chitter-chattered something that sounded quite evil.

And then . . .

. . . with a wave of his evil paw and a flash . . .

. . . Noah created a huge

cloud of smoke and then there was a . . .

CHAPTER 8

The Trail Ends

And somehow Milton's mother was teleported out of the classroom.

Milton knew enough about teleporting that he was sure his mother was okay wherever she was. The big problem was figuring out: Where was she?

Noah giggled a sinister giggle before scampering away down the hall.

"Follow that ferret!" Milton declared.

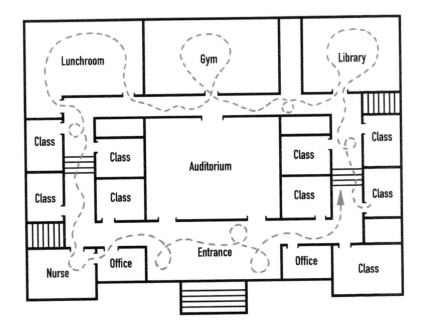

Milton chased Noah up a staircase and then down another. Around the library, through the gym and the lunchroom, down the hall into the nurse's office, across the main entrance, and up the same staircase.

Wow, Noah's just going in circles, Milton thought.

But what Milton didn't know was that ferrets like going in circles. It's how they get away from bigger animals—like Milton!

After about eight laps around the school—when Milton thought he just might collapse from running—Noah changed course and scurried down the dimly lit stairway into the basement.

It was in the dark basement that Milton finally lost Noah. The ferret's trail ended at a room with a door clearly marked . . .

Milton had seen that door before. The sign had always stopped him from going inside. But this time, he realized that the first letters of the words *No One Allowed Here* were *N . . . O . . . A . . . H.*

Noah!

Milton peeked through the small window in the door. He saw . . .

. . . Noah and all the pets from the other classrooms together.

"Howie the hedgehog is now hateful! Lawrence the lizard is loathsome! Crosby the crab is cranky! Roger the rat is ridiculously rotten!" Milton said, unaware that he was putting Mrs. Baltman's recent alliteration lesson to good use.

Then Milton noticed a person on a chair in the corner of the room. It was his mom! Noah had MegaGlued her to the chair!

"Oh no! This isn't good," Milton said. "No, this isn't good at all."

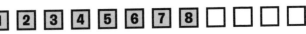

You've read eight whole chapters. That's amazing!

1 2 3 4 5 6 7 8 ☐ ☐ ☐ ☐

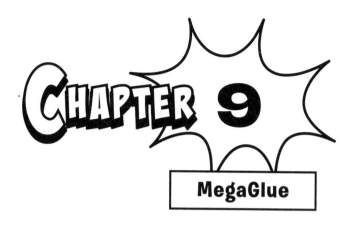

CHAPTER 9

MegaGlue

Milton watched as Noah looked at Mrs. Worthy and said, "Chit-chatter-chit-chatter-chit-chatter-grump!"

Somehow, Milton's mom was able to understand Noah. She replied . . .

"What do you mean: Today the school, tonight the town?"

Noah giggled a sinister giggle and said, "Errp-chat-chitter-chatter-errp-blotz-blotz."

"Yes, of course my ring is a ferret decoder.

It's standard issue. You know that! So now you tell me: What do you mean that the Society of Substitutes can't stop you this time?"

Noah said, "Grump-blotz-chatter-chit-errp."

Milton knew he had to do something, but he also knew he'd need help. He tiptoed back upstairs to Room 311B. The classroom was empty. Incredibly, outdoor recess was *still* going on.

Milton wasn't sure what to do. He knew that he probably didn't have much time to save his mom. Or the school. Or the town. Or the world.

And, oh yeah, the final episode of *Wow! That's Talent.*

So, figuring that two heads were better than a

whole bunch of animal heads, Milton asked his best pal to help him.

"Pssst, Morgan," Milton called out to her from inside the classroom. "Please come here."

Morgan had been playing badminton. But she called time-out and joined Milton in the doorway.

"What's up, Milton?" Morgan asked. "Where ya been?"

"It's a long, weird story."

"Milton, I'm your best friend. You can tell me."

"Okay. But you won't believe this."

Milton shared everything, as fast and as clearly as he could.

MRS. BALTMAN. NOAH ESCAPED. FAKE COUGHING. MY MOM SUBSTITUTES.

"I *knew* it was a fake cough," Morgan told him.

"There's more. Blueprints. Questions about Noah—"

"Yeah, so? That just tells me that your mom wants us to find Noah!" Morgan replied.

"But Noah is *evil*."

"*Evil?* Do you mean the time he scratched Max? That was an accident!"

"Not talking about a scratch!" Milton insisted. "Noah is a sinister ferret! With sinister plans!"

"*What?*"

"Our class ferret wants to teleport the whole town to an evil island!"

"That's ridiculous!"

Milton continued telling Morgan everything that had happened. He even showed her his mom's S.O.S. superhero helmet—which she quickly tried on.

Morgan thought it looked awesome on her. But when she went to put it back in the charger, the microphone cracked. Morgan grabbed the MegaGlue, but Milton told her there wasn't time to repair the helmet.

So she stuffed the glue in her pocket as they ran off...

... to save the world!

Num-Nums

Morgan and Milton left Room 311B and headed toward the animals' basement headquarters. Acting like superheroes from their favorite movies, the pair slithered and sleuthed around corners.

"We need a plan," Morgan told Milton as they got to the stairs leading to the basement. "Good superheroes have plans."

"Right," Milton told her. "We gotta stop this evil, num-num-loving ferret."

"Num-nums! *That's it!*" Morgan exclaimed.

"Huh? What do you mean?" Milton asked.

"Well, if there's one thing classroom pets enjoy more than world domination, it's their num-nums," Morgan told him.

"We'll distract them with num-nums!" Milton said, looking in his sweatshirt pocket. "Buffalo-flavor num-nums, if I'm not mistaken."

"Come on, let's go rescue your superhero

substitute mom!" Morgan said.

The kids scurried down the stairs.

When they reached the basement, Milton pointed to many extra pet cages that had been stored downstairs. Morgan nodded.

Working quickly and quietly, Morgan and Milton arranged the cages outside the animals' headquarters. They left the cage doors open, and they dabbed them with the MegaGlue from Morgan's pocket.

Next, Milton quietly opened the door to the animals' headquarters and pulled out the chicken wings he'd packed in his sweatshirt pocket.

"Num-nums!" he shouted. "Come and get them!"

Sniffing the food, Noah and the other animals stopped their meeting and zoomed toward the yummy treats. Milton and Morgan tossed the chicken wings into the empty pet cages.

The animals raced into their cages.

They were so busy eating the delicious chicken wing treats that they didn't even notice that the cage doors had all snapped closed behind them. With the MegaGlue holding the doors firmly shut, the evil animals were once again safely behind bars!

"Mission accomplished!" Milton and Morgan said as they high-fived each other with hands that were still orange and greasy from the chicken wing sauce.

But before they could finish their elaborate fist-bump, elbow-slap, spin, twist, booty-shake high five, they heard a panicked voice yell out from the darkness.

It was Milton's mom—and she was still in trouble.

**Only two more chapters to go.
How do you think this will end?**

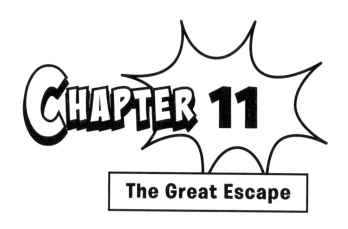

The Great Escape

Milton and Morgan ran into the room marked *No One Allowed Here.*

"I'm trapped!" Mrs. Worthy yelled out. "Help!" Noah had MegaGlued Milton's mom to a chair.

The empty Mega-Glue tube was on the floor. Milton grabbed it and read the label.

"'This is the very best product on Earth,'" he read aloud to his mom and Morgan. "And it says that they promise that MegaGlue is the only glue that stays stuck no matter what."

"No matter what?" Morgan asked.

"No matter what," he repeated.

"Oh, Milton!" his mother said. "Don't worry, I won't be stuck to this chair forever. We just need to think!"

"Superheroes may not run in my family,"

Morgan said, "but I think I might have a pretty super idea!"

"Tell us!" Mrs. Worthy said.

"If you look closely, you'll see that *only your sweater* is glued to the chair," Morgan pointed out.

"You're right! That's wonderful! Morgan Zhou, I hereby name you an honorary superhero substitute teacher!" Milton's mother told her.

"Thank you," Morgan said. "Though could I be a superhero *without* being a substitute teacher?"

"Of course," Mrs. Worthy told her. "But I have to tell you, being a sub is the best thing about being part of the S.O.S."

Mrs. Worthy then took off her sweater and led the kids out of the room.

NO
ONE
ALLOWED
HERE

She slammed the door so hard, the *No One Allowed Here* sign fell off.

"So *that's* 311A!" Milton exclaimed.

As they walked away, Mrs. Worthy laughed and waved at Noah.

"Chitter-errp-blotz-mucky-freg-freg!" she told the ferret.

It's a good thing that her decoder ring allowed her to speak ferret as well as she understood it.

It's also probably a good thing that *you* don't speak ferret.

SuperTurboDrive

Moments later, Milton's mom was back to simply being Mrs. Worthy. She was glad to be standing in front of the classroom, teaching just as any nonsuperhero substitute teacher might.

The kids were all hot, tired, and sweaty after two whole morning recesses. David Tessler went to sneak a quick snack and was shocked to find all his chicken wings were gone. But they all agreed it was good to finally get to sit down and that lunchtime couldn't come soon enough.

Later that day, Milton's mom told him that Noah was coming back to the classroom. Learning about Milton's and Morgan's heroism, Chief Chiefman thought Room 311B was the safest place to keep him. To prepare for his arrival, the class built a brand-new escape-proof cage. They made sure the door would close and lock by itself in case someone (such as Milton)

accidentally left it open again.

Once the cage was ready, Mrs. Worthy called the office and Andy the janitor brought Noah back to class.

Noah seemed calm. His expression said, *I'm sorry.* But was he? No one knew for sure.

But when they transferred him to his new cage, Milton's mom sighed a big sigh of relief.

For the moment, the world was safe again.

Milton and Morgan were glad to learn that the other classroom animals had all been happily returned to their cages. They were back to being adorable, well-loved classroom pets.

Brrrrrrrrrrrrring!

Milton exhaled. To him, the bell that ended the school day could not come soon enough.

But . . . that *brrrrrrrrrrrrrring* had not been the school bell. It was David Tessler tossing the spoons and forks out of his backpack as he searched for his delicious missing chicken wings.

"Where, oh, where are they?" he cried.

However, just a moment or two later, the school bell *did* ring. And the students in Room 311B got up to leave. It had been a very tiring, very strange day.

By tomorrow, life would be back to normal. Well, for everyone *except* Milton, who had learned that his mother was a superhero.

"Come on, kid," Milton's mother said. "Let's go home."

Once they were both safely buckled in, Milton's mom began driving. She looked at her son in the rearview mirror.

"Thank you for helping to save me today."

"No problemo, Mom," Milton said.

"I know you're probably wondering about all that happened. I'll be glad to answer anything you want to know," Milton's mom said.

"Actually, I do have a million billion questions," he told her. "Maybe even a million billion and seven. But for now, there's only one thing I would really like to ask you."

"Of course, my son. What do you want to know?"

"Mom, if you're a real-life superhero . . ."

"Yes?"

"Can you fly?"

Milton's mom smiled.

"No," she said. "I *can't* fly. But we need to get out of this traffic soon. If we don't, we'll be eating dinner so late that we might miss the final episode of *Wow! That's Talent!*"

"You're right," Milton replied.

Then, just like that, Mrs. Worthy put the SUV into SuperTurboDrive . . .

. . . and it took off, up into the air, soaring high above the school buses, the trees, and the good students of Beacher Elementary School.

The end.

(For now.)

1 2 3 4 5 6 7 8 9 10 11 12

CONGRATULATIONS!

You've read **12** chapters,

87 pages,

and **5,037** words!

All your super-sleuthing paid off!

SUPER AWESOME GAMES

Think

Mrs. Worthy has a lot of cool gadgets to help fight the bad guys. If you could have any cool crime-fighting gadget,  what would it be? Draw it on a piece of notebook paper.

Feel

Milton was surprised when he learned that his mother was going to be his substitute teacher. Can you think of a  time when you were surprised by something someone you know did? Can you turn that moment into a short comic?

Act

In this story, Mrs. Worthy uses a blueprint of the school to figure out  where Noah might be hiding. A blueprint is a lot like a map. Can you draw a map of your home and school? Label all the places that are important to you.

Alan Katz has written more than forty books, including *Take Me Out of the Bathtub and Other Silly Dilly Songs*, *The Day the Mustache Took Over*, *OOPS!*, and *Really Stupid Stories for Really Smart Kids*. He has received many awards for his writing, and he loves visiting schools across the country.

Alex Lopez was born in Sabadell, a city in Spain near Barcelona. Alex has always loved to draw. His work has been featured in many books in many countries, but nowadays, he focuses mostly on illustrating books for young readers and teens.